Charles M. Schulz

Aaugh! A Dog Ate My Book Report

📚 HarperCollins®

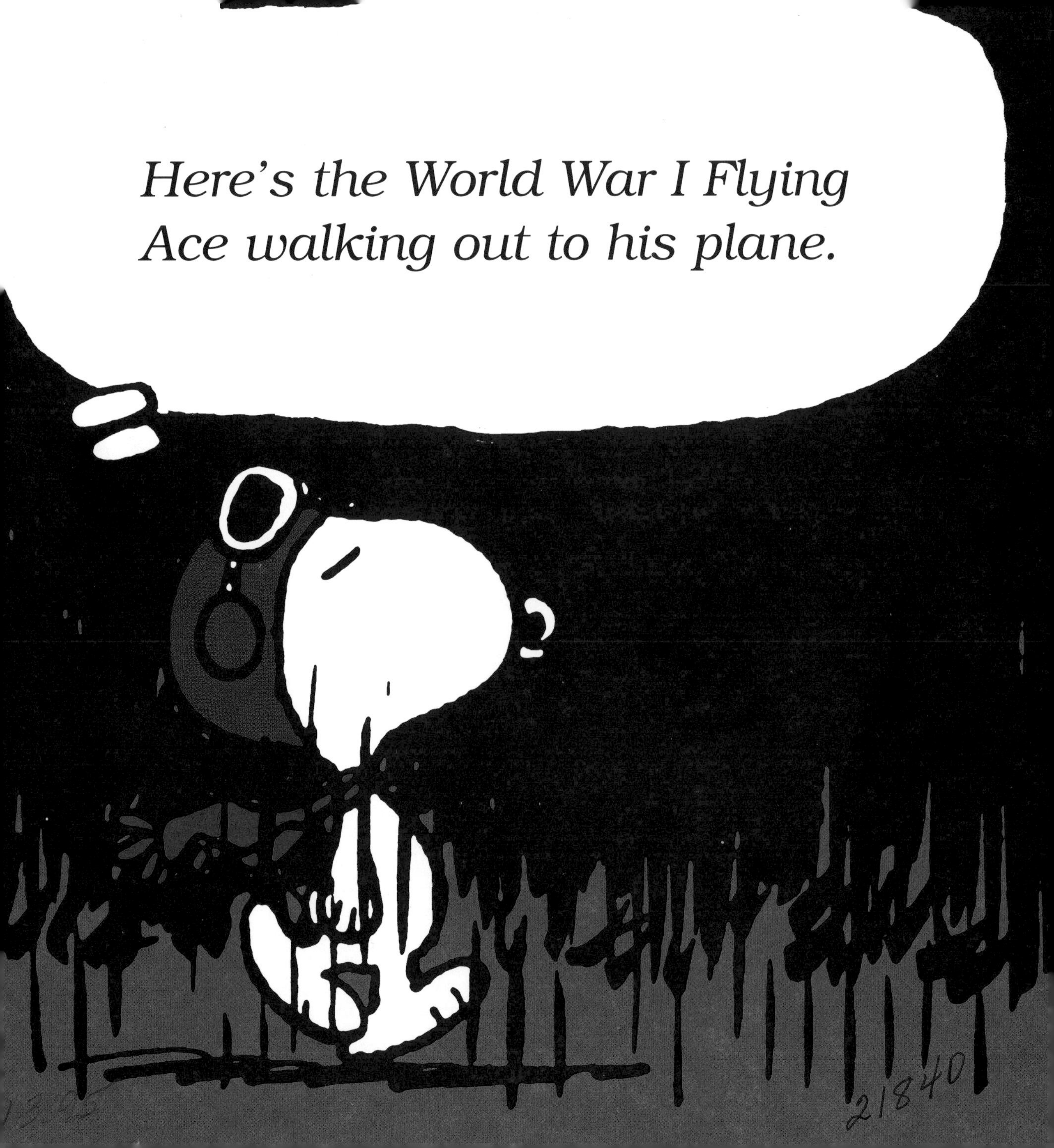
Here's the World War I Flying Ace walking out to his plane.

It is dawn . . . a light mist is falling. Our squadron commander says this will be a perfect day for a surprise attack.

Here's the World War I Flying Ace zooming through the air in his Sopwith Camel. Those poor soldiers down there in the trenches hate me.

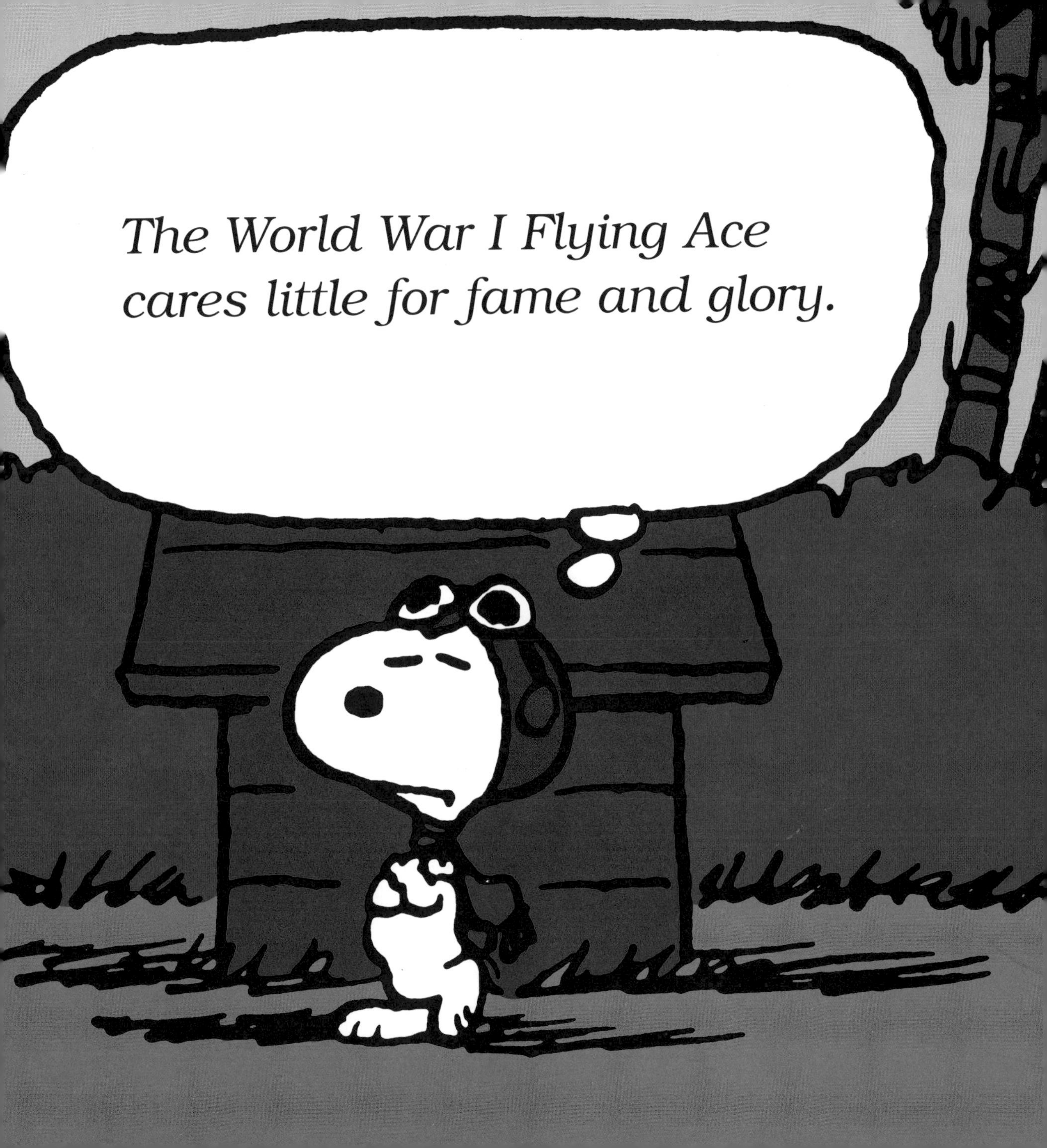
The World War I Flying Ace cares little for fame and glory.

His only wish is to do his duty, serve with honor, and perhaps be called "Stout Fellow."

"Fat."

"What are you doing up so early?"

"I had to finish this report for school."

"If I don't get it in today, I'm doomed!"

Here's the World War I Flying Ace down behind enemy lines. His mission is to get the secret papers. Suddenly, he sees her . . .

"Hey! What are you doing?
That's my book report!!!"

Not fooled by the girl's simple cries, the Flying Ace darts swiftly away!

"You stupid beagle! Come back here with my book report!"

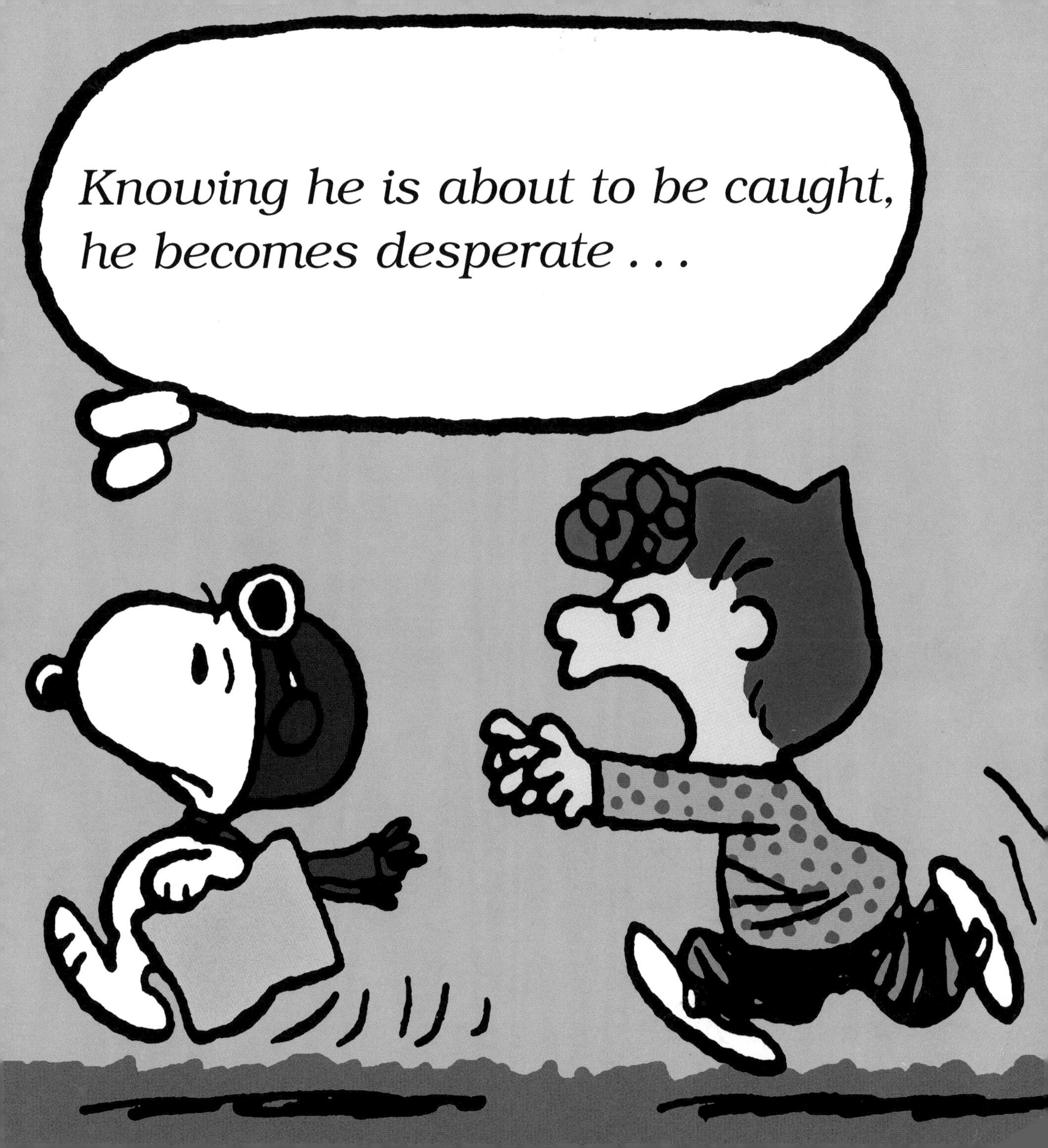
Knowing he is about to be caught,
he becomes desperate . . .

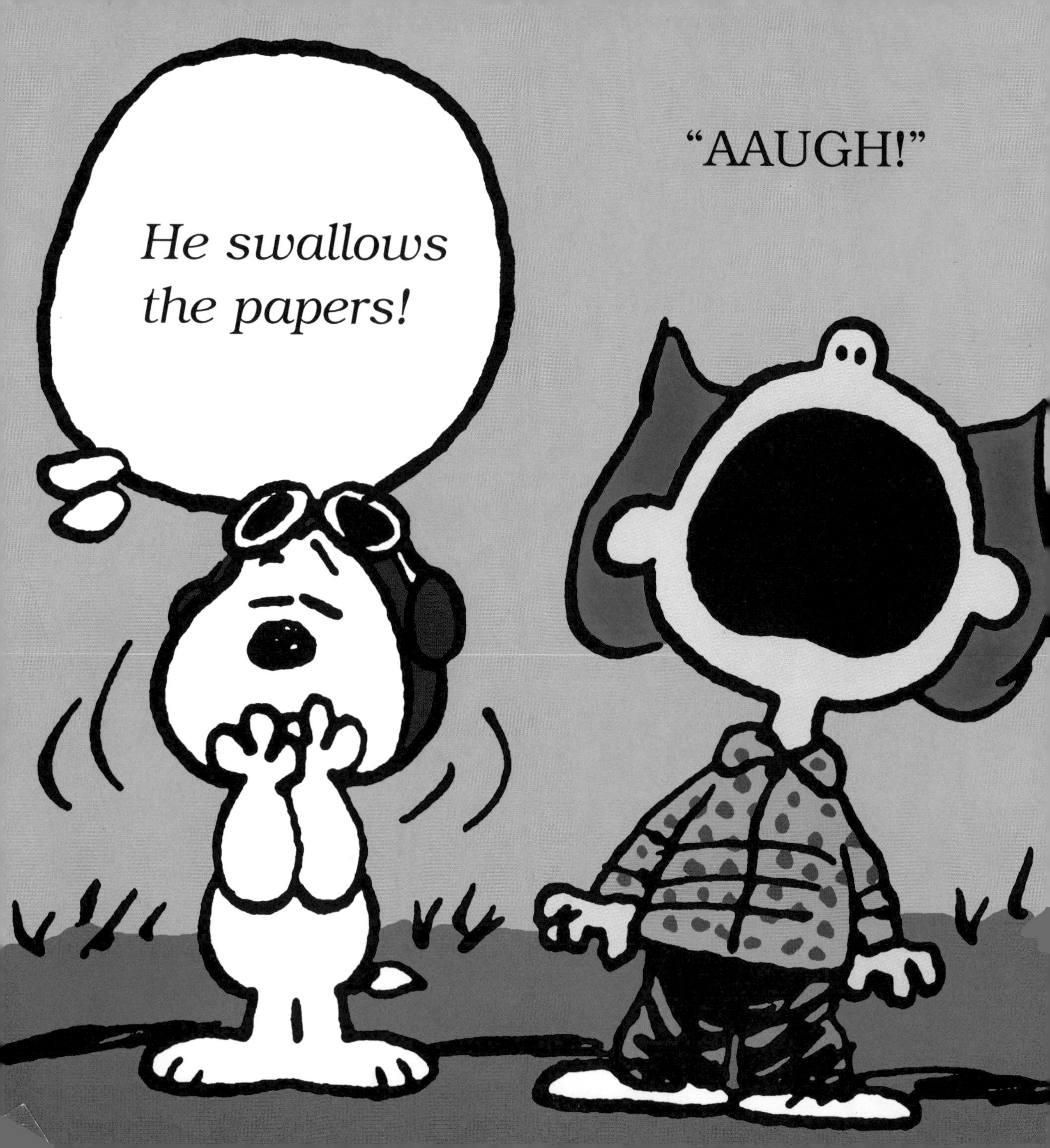
He swallows the papers!
"AAUGH!"

"You stupid beagle! You swallowed my book report!"

"Sorry I'm late, Ma'am. I had a little problem with my book report."

"Anyway, here it is!"

"Yes, Ma'am? You want me to read my book report to the class?"

Oh, no!

"Well, I may have a little difficulty reading it."

"However, I'll see what I can remember."

Just hit the high points.